Born to Run

and other sports stories

by

Mark Phialas

Watermill Press

Illustrations by Jim Odbert

ISBN 0-89375-742-X

Contents

The Missing Helmets

"Twenty-two Dive!" Coach Thompson shouted. "And try blocking this time!"

The quarterback took the snap from center, faked a pitch-out to his halfback, and neatly tucked the ball into the arms of the fullback. A solid wall of defensive players held position and slammed the ball carrier to the turf.

"Where's the blocking?" screamed Coach Thompson. "Take a break."

Mitch Robinson passed out orange slices to the squad. Mitch was too small to play on the team, so he had become the manager. It was his job to make sure the squad had everything it needed. It was not a hero's role, but it was an important part in the machinery of a team.

"This has been a lousy practice," Coach Thompson said. "You guys have a chance for the greatest season in the history of Jefferson High School. But if you lose tomorrow, it will be just another night we give Jordan the title."

Silence fell upon the Bulldogs. Coach Thompson was right. They had played lousy.

A solid wall of defensive players held position.

Then, the team began to chant, "Jefferson . . . Jefferson . . . Jefferson."

"That's the spirit," smiled Coach Thompson. "Try 22 Dive again."

This time the right guard blocked the middle linebacker, allowing the fullback to run for a big gain.

"Yeah!" Mitch yelled. With plays like that, Jefferson would have a chance.

After practice, Mitch arranged the team's uniforms for the contest against Jordan. First, he packed the jerseys, shoulder pads, and pants. Next, he stacked the helmets in a large duffel bag. He placed the equipment near the locker room door. The next afternoon, he would load it onto the bus.

Then Mitch threw the team's practice uniforms into another bag. A local laundry would pick them up in the morning.

The next afternoon, Mitch loaded the activity bus with the equipment. The Bulldogs climbed into the bus, buzzing with excitement.

The old bus had broken down many times. It coughed and wheezed on the highway. But at last they arrived at Jordan Stadium.

A huge burst of steam came out of the engine, and the bus sagged to a halt. A crowd of Jordan fans laughed.

"Don't worry about them," Coach Thompson said. "We'll warm up and then return to the locker room for a meeting."

The Bulldogs had a great warm-up. Then, in the locker room, Coach Thompson told the team he was proud of them. There was a half-hour until game time.

"OK, Mitch," said the coach. "Give

them their helmets."

Mitch picked up the duffel bag. It felt strange. And when he looked inside, he quivered.

"Uh, I guess I brought the wrong bag," Mitch stammered. "We don't have any helmets."

Coach Thompson grabbed the duffel bag and turned it over. Instead of helmets, uniforms fell on the floor. Everyone groaned.

"That bus will never make it back to school in time," Coach Thompson said, glaring at Mitch. "We'll have to forfeit, unless we can talk Jordan into postponing the game. We can't play without helmets."

A large tackle picked Mitch up by his shirt.

"You ought to be strangled," the tackle muttered.

A large tackle picked Mitch up by his shirt.

Mitch ran out of the locker room. At first, he ran just to get away. But then, he saw a police car and had an idea.

"Help!" Mitch yelled as he ran toward the cruiser. He told the officer his story about the missing helmets.

"This is Jordan territory," the officer said. "Not too many people would mind if you had to forfeit."

Mitch wanted to find a large rock to crawl under.

"But, as it happens, I went to school at Jefferson," the officer said. "Get in."

In a matter of moments, the police car was in the Jefferson parking lot. Mitch raced into the gym to get the other duffel bag. But it was gone. He saw a laundry tag on the floor.

Suddenly, Mitch knew the laundry service had taken the wrong bag.

He ran back to the police car. As the

car sped towards the laundry, Mitch saw a laundry truck parked on the side of the road, with a flat tire.

Please be the right truck, Mitch begged silently. Then he yelled, "Did you pick up laundry at Jefferson this morning?"

The man fixing the tire nodded.

"I'll explain later," Mitch said as he hopped into the truck. In the far corner, he saw a duffel bag with the initials "JHS."

"I've got them," Mitch shouted as he ran back to the car.

It was time for the kick-off as the police car approached the stadium. With lights flashing and the siren on full blast, the officer drove to the center of the field. Mitch leaped out of the cruiser with the duffel bag.

"You don't have to forfeit," Mitch

said. And as he emptied the bag, helmets poured onto the field.

"Does this mean you're ready to play?" asked the head official.

"You bet it does," Coach Thompson said.

All the excitement gave the Bulldogs an extra edge. They clobbered Jordan 21–0, to win their first league championship.

Coach Thompson and the squad found out that the laundry had caused the mix-up. They had picked up the wrong bag. And it was Mitch's quick thinking that had saved the day.

"Usually, we award a game ball to our most valuable player," Coach Thompson shouted above the noisy celebration in the locker room. "But this is a special occasion. Mitch, I am proud to present you with a game helmet."

"Mitch, I am proud to present you with a game helmet."

Mitch blushed as he put on his trophy. The team picked him up and tossed him into the showers.

After all, heroes always get tossed into the showers.

Hit or Miss

"All right, gang," Coach Jones said. "Gather round and meet a new Dodger, Dave Holmes."

"Hi," Dave said as the Dodgers looked him over. Finally, Eddie Watson, the captain, stuck out his hand.

"I'm Eddie," he said. "What position do you like to play?"

"Second base," said Dave.

"I cover shortstop," Eddie said. Eddie's closest friend, Tom Hankins, played second base.

"Are you new in town?" Eddie asked Dave as they went towards the field to practice.

"We just moved here," Dave said.

Coach Jones blew his whistle. "Let's have a little infield practice," he called out to the team. "Dave, you watch Eddie and Tom for a while. And then, we'll see what you can do at second base."

Dave was used to waiting, and he sat patiently on the bench. He was a good fielder, but he had always been inconsistent as a hitter. He wanted to improve at both hitting and fielding.

Eddie and Tom worked very well at their positions. They shared a smooth easy style that proved they had played together a long time. Eddie scooped up a grounder and tossed it to Tom. Tom made a quick pivot after planting a foot on the bag and fired a strike to Jeremy at first base.

"That's the way to operate!" yelled a Dodger from the outfield.

Later, Dave got his chance to perform on the field. As he trotted towards second base, he noticed a strange look on Eddie's face.

"OK, new kid," Eddie muttered. "Let's see if you can play ball."

Dave winced at this. For some reason, Eddie was not too friendly.

Dave began searching the playing area for pebbles and anything else that might cause the ball to bounce. This was a habit of Dave's. He found two or three small stones, picked them up, and tossed them towards the outfield.

"Are you looking for clues, Sherlock

Holmes?" Eddie said, just loud enough for Dave to hear.

Coach Jones hit a hard, bouncing ball to Eddie, who played it on the third hop and tossed it to Dave at second. Dave stepped on the bag and rifled it to first base. A few moments later, Dave cruised behind second base to barely stab the ball with his glove. As he was falling off balance, he managed to underhand the ball to Eddie at the bag.

"Nice work!" Coach Jones said. "Batting practice."

As each of the Dodgers took a turn at the plate, Dave could tell that Eddie and Tom were the best hitters on the squad. Dave did not do very well at bat. He hit several slow rollers and a couple of pop flies. Only one line drive to the outfield would have been a hit.

The Dodgers played two games that

*Dave cruised behind second base to barely
stab the ball with his glove.*

week and won them both. Eddie hit two home runs while Tom went six for seven. Defensively, they turned five double plays.

Dave played only in the last inning of the second game. He didn't get a chance to field a ball or hit, but he did cheer a lot.

The following week, the Dodgers faced the White Sox. In the fourth inning, Tom smashed a line drive to left center. Trying for extra bases, Tom turned his ankle and had to limp off the field.

"Give it a shot, Dave," Coach Jones said to his new second baseman. Eagerly, Dave grabbed his glove and raced onto the playing field, catching a sharp look from Eddie.

"Don't mess up, new kid," Eddie mumbled.

But that's just what Dave did. In the

next inning, Dave let an easy ground ball get past him, allowing two White Sox to score. He struck out three times as well. And each time he struck out, there were Dodgers in scoring position. The Dodgers lost the ball game 2–0.

Dave felt miserable. To make matters worse, Eddie barked at Dave in front of the rest of the team.

"Tom had better be able to play soon. We don't seem to have anyone else who can cover second and hit!"

"Cool it, Watson!" Coach Jones said sharply. "And Holmes, don't let it get to you. Even Bobby Richardson had some bad days at second base."

Tom's ankle was only slightly twisted, and he was able to play the next game. Dave stayed on the bench, hoping to get another chance.

The Dodgers faced the Pirates for the

Dave struck out three times.

second time of the season. The Pirates had won the first contest quite easily, and now, they held a 3–1 lead in the fifth inning.

One of the Pirates cracked a grounder towards Tom. The ball skipped at the last moment, hitting Tom full in the face. Immediately, his face began to swell and his right eye closed.

"Oh no!" Eddie said as Dave trotted onto the field to replace Tom. "It's all over now."

"I can play," Dave said. "Just give me a chance."

"You had your chance," said Eddie. "Why don't you go swat some flies?"

Dave charged towards Eddie, ready to fight for a little respect. But the umpire at second base stepped between Eddie and Dave.

"Save it for the Pirates," the ump

said. "This is a ballgame, not a fight."

Dave went back to his position, talking to himself. In the sixth inning, when he came to bat, he was still fuming. He was intent upon proving to Eddie and the whole team that he could do the job.

Dave gave full concentration to each pitch. He swung smoothly on a high curve and hit a crisp single to left field. As he stood grinning on first base, the Dodgers cheered.

"That's the way, Sherlock!" Like Eddie, some of the Dodgers called Dave "Sherlock," because his last name was Holmes. Also, Dave was always snooping around the infield, looking for pebbles and stones.

Eddie came to bat. He promptly slammed the first pitch towards center field. The ball sailed over the fence, hitting a clothesline across the street.

Dave and Eddie waltzed around the bases, tying the contest 3–3.

In the seventh inning, the Pirates threatened to reclaim the lead. They had two runners in scoring position, with two outs. One of the Pirates tapped a slow roller towards Dave. Dave charged the ball and fired his throw to home plate, ending the Pirate rally.

"Not bad, Sherlock," Eddie admitted.

In the eighth inning, the Dodgers scored and led 4–3. But in the top of the ninth, the Pirates came back with two runs of their own, grabbing a 5–4 lead.

The Dodgers had one final chance in the bottom of the ninth. With two outs, they began to rally. A single and a double put runners on second and third. And now, it was Dave's turn to hit.

Dave tried to relax. He told himself

that it was just another hit-or-miss situation. But he knew a lot more was at stake. He swung on the first pitch, a fast ball, and missed. As he moved out of the batter's box to calm his nerves, Eddie's voice rang across the diamond.

"Come on, Sherlock! You can do it!"

Dave took the next pitch for a ball. With a 1–1 count, he slashed a line drive to right center. The ball sailed through the gap, and the Dodger base runners easily scored. The Dodgers won the ball game 6–5.

The squad rushed at Dave. They grabbed him and hoisted him up on their shoulders, yelling at the top of their lungs. Eddie walked over to Dave after things died down a bit.

"I was wrong, Sherlock. You've got the stuff to play. I was just giving you a hard time. But I'm real glad you got

With a 1–1 count, Dave slashed a line drive.

that hit!"

"That's OK, Doctor," Dave said.

"What did you call me?" wondered Eddie.

"You guys call me Sherlock because my last name is Holmes and I'm always snooping around for things," explained Dave. "Well, I'm calling you Doctor because your last name is Watson. And your cheering is good for my health."

And that's how Holmes and Watson, for the second time, became a great combination.

Double Fault

"It's your serve!" Steve yelled across the net.

"All right," Betty said. She tossed a tennis ball high into the air. Arching and twisting her back, she prepared to hit the ball. At the proper moment, her body uncoiled, her wrist snapped, and her racket smacked the ball very hard.

*Betty smacked the ball very hard
with her racket.*

Steve never had a chance as Betty's serve flew past him. It was another ace, one of many that she hit that afternoon. Betty hit her next serve a fraction out and had to hit a second ball. She used a spin serve, controlling the ball to make sure it would be in.

Steve hit a firm backhand return, but Betty charged the net, volleying the ball past Steve for a winner. Two points later, she took the set 6–0.

"Nice match," Steve said. "I guess I'll see you later."

Steve's shoulders slumped as he left the court. Betty watched him, thinking how nice he was. Steve wasn't that great at tennis, but tennis wasn't everything.

How come he never asks me out? Betty thought.

When she arrived at home, Betty had

a surprise. Her brother, Nathan, was home from college. He was shooting baskets next door.

"Hey, hey, hey!" Nathan called. "Did you lose or what? You don't look so hot."

Betty shrugged and wandered into the house. Upstairs in her room, she turned on her stereo and sat on her rug, brooding about Steve.

Nathan knocked on her door and said, "I just wanted to say hi before I head back to the dorm."

"Come on in," said Betty. Nathan was a sophomore at college, and though he didn't know as much as he thought he did, he could be really nice sometimes.

"Just as I thought," Nathan said when he saw Betty. "You look like you've got the blues. What's the story?"

"It's Steve," Betty said, her voice

"How come he never asks me out?"
wondered Betty.

trembling. "He doesn't even know I'm alive."

Betty looked out her window, hiding a tear that had trickled down her cheek.

"You're feeling pretty sorry for yourself, aren't you?" Nathan said. "That's got to stop. By the way, do you *always* win when you play against Steve?"

"Yeah," said Betty.

"How badly do you beat him?"

"I usually win all of the games," she said.

"Well, no wonder he's not so friendly," Nathan said. "You've hurt his pride. Maybe he thinks that if he can't impress you with his tennis, you wouldn't be interested in him at all."

Betty leaped to her feet in Steve's defense. "That's not true at all. He's absolutely terrific!"

"Let him know it," Nathan said. "I'll

see you later."

Betty felt a lot better when she came up with a plan for her next tennis encounter with Steve. Three days later, they played tennis again.

Betty served first, and double-faulted the first two points. Trailing love–30, she hit a spin serve to Steve's forehand. Steve pounced on the ball, ripping a winner across court. Betty double-faulted again, allowing Steve to win the game at love.

Steve hit his usual half-speed serve. Betty could always handle it with ease, but today, she clubbed the ball almost over the fence.

"Are you alright?" asked Steve.

"It's not my day," Betty said. She lost that game, and when it was her turn to serve, she double-faulted again.

Steve tossed his racket towards the

Steve pounced on the ball.

edge of the court. "I've had it," he said. "You're not trying at all. I don't know why you want me to win, but I'm not a charity case."

Betty looked at Steve. She didn't know what to do. Finally, she walked towards him.

"You're right," she said. "I was missing on purpose. I thought if you won a few games, you'd like me better."

"Like you? I think you're great!"

"But. . ."

"I guess I'm shy," Steve said. "Tennis was the only way I was sure you'd see me. Heck, I'm lousy at tennis, but tennis isn't everything, is it?"

"I like movies," Betty said with a smile. "And music, and dancing, and...and I think you're great, too."

Steve cleared his throat. "Well, what are you doing Friday night?" he asked.

"Going to a movie with you?"

"You got it," Steve said. "But no more double-faults, OK?"

"OK," Betty said. "We've had enough tennis anyway."

Nathan is right about one thing, thought Betty. *You've got to let people know what you feel.*

Too-Tall Joan

"Have you got everything?"

"Yes, Mother," Joan said. She usually had everything, but her mother always asked, just the same.

"Remember to stand up straight," her mother added.

Joan cringed. She was tired of that subject. She had grown seven inches in the past year, and now she had a problem with her posture. Towering above her friends, Joan slumped to feel not quite so tall.

Mary Hankins met Joan at the bus stop. They were best friends and wanted to go to the same university to study medicine.

"Did you finish the lab project for biology?" asked Mary. Mary was as short as Joan was tall.

"Yeah, the only thing I'm not ready for is gym class."

"Joan, you're never ready for that," Mary giggled.

Later, in gym class, Joan and Mary stood in a long line of girls. Today, they were being introduced to the fundamentals of volleyball.

"What are we supposed to do?" Joan said.

Joan and Mary stood in a long line of girls.

"Try to hit the ball to the other side of the net," Mary said eagerly.

A volleyball flew towards Joan, colliding with her unready hands and falling to the floor.

"What are you doing, Joan?" asked Mrs. Fielding, the gym instructor.

"Nothing, Mrs. Fielding," Joan replied.

"That's so true," Mrs. Fielding said. "You've got to play the ball. Don't let the ball play you. With your height, you've got a great advantage."

"Yes," Joan said, staring at the floor.

"You're interested in passing this course, aren't you?"

"Yes."

"Then, try again," Mrs. Fielding said. "This time, approach the ball with the idea of sending it across the net. That *is* the point to this game."

Joan blushed. She felt ten feet tall because she knew everyone was looking at her. She missed the ball completely, and the class howled with laughter. On her third try, Joan made contact with the ball, sending it high into the rafters.

"Better," Mrs. Fielding said with a pain in her voice. "Next."

Mary bent her knees as the ball neared her, and timed the shot perfectly.

"Nice shot. Take note of that, Joan," Mrs. Fielding barked.

After school, Joan and Mary walked home together.

"Wow, did I mess up in gym class," Joan said with a sigh. "What's wrong with me?"

"Nothing," Mary said. "You can do anything you want to. The only difference between you and the others is how

45

*Joan made contact with the ball, sending it
high into the rafters.*

you feel about yourself. Sometimes, I think you'd like to be my height."

"Yes, a thousand times yes!"

"For a long time," Mary said, "I wanted to be tall just like you. But that's something I couldn't change. So I decided to be the best me that I could possibly be. Now I like who I am. But you don't really like yourself, do you?"

Joan thought about what Mary had said. *I've got to learn to like myself*, she thought.

Later, at home, she found a magazine, "For Tall Girls Only," in the den. Joan took the magazine to her room and read every article. She really liked a story about tall girls who model, and how most of the models had been embarrassed about their height. Yet, these girls had learned to accept their height and use it to good advantage.

"I've got to give this a try," Joan said with determination.

The next morning, she hopped out of bed, taking her time getting dressed. Finally, she chose the outfit that made her feel the most beautiful.

"Have you got...?"

"Yes, Mother, I've got it all," Joan said, gracefully walking out the front door. On the way to school, Joan thought about gym class. She decided to have a better attitude. Standing tall, she would do her best in volleyball.

In gym class, that afternoon, Joan could hardly wait to get started. When the ball came to her, she bent her knees like Mary, concentrated, and hit the ball perfectly.

"Terrific, Joan," Mrs. Fielding said cheerfully. "You look interested today."

"I am."

Joan spiked the ball.

"I would like to see you play the net."

Joan moved closer to the net. In this position, her height gave her an advantage over the other players.

"Set her up, Mary," Mrs. Fielding said.

Mary tossed the volleyball high above Joan's head. Joan, stretching to her full height, leaped and spiked the ball.

"Wow!" said Mary.

"That's the way, Joan!" Mrs. Fielding yelled. "How about coming to the volleyball team tryouts today?"

"I guess I'm tall enough," Joan said with pride. Now, she felt tall enough to do anything.

Hold 'Em, Tiger!

When the final bell rang, Bill Harris grabbed his books and hurried outside to find Joe Morton. They had had an argument at lunch, and now they were going to settle things.

Bill turned the corner of the building and found Joe waiting for him. Joe weighed nearly 170 pounds and was pretty strong. Bill, on the other hand, was rather small, weighing only 95 pounds. But the difference in size didn't matter to Bill. He was tired of having Joe Morton shove his weight around.

They tossed their books onto the ground and charged headfirst into each other. They struggled and rolled on the ground, until they heard a whistle.

Coach Harding separated the two fighters. "I saw you guys at lunch, and I knew you'd be at it again. Come with me to my office."

Bill and Joe trudged behind Coach Harding. They had been caught fighting on school grounds and would probably be in a lot of trouble. But Coach Harding surprised them.

"I'm not going to report this, but you have to do something for me."

"What?" asked Bill.

"I want you to put all of that energy to good use. I think you'd both make good wrestlers."

"Wrestling is fake," Bill said. "It's just a bunch of clowns in tiger suits, beating their chests."

Coach Harding laughed. "Professional wrestling may be fake, but amateur wrestling is very much for real. Wrestling is a team sport, Bill. And it needs people in good condition who aren't afraid of hard work."

"How can it be a team sport?" Joe asked.

"Come to practice and find out," said the coach.

The next afternoon, Bill and Joe listened to Coach Harding talk about wrestling. They watched as he demonstrated some basic moves. Bill liked what he heard. He had always

"How can it be a team sport?" Joe asked.

wanted to be part of a team.

"Wrestlers must be smart and be able to adapt to unexpected situations," Coach Harding said. "Most important, you must be in excellent condition to wrestle."

Bill found out about conditioning in his first practice bout. After just a few minutes on the mat, he was panting, coughing, and out of breath.

Coach Harding passed around some written information about wrestling. Bill learned that there are weight divisions in wrestling. In each division, a wrestler could weigh a maximum amount. If he weighed more than the maximum amount, he would have to wrestle in a heavier weight division.

"Weight divisions make sure wrestlers are evenly matched in size and strength. This means skill and desire determine the better wrestler," Coach Harding explained.

Bill wrestled in the 95-pound weight class. Joe was placed in the 175-pound division. Wrestling practice was hard work. But soon, they were ready for their first match against Fairview, the defending champs.

Bill was the lightest wrestler on the squad, so he wrestled first. When he took off his sweat clothes, he felt a little silly in his tights. But tights were better than tiger suits and pirate costumes.

Bill moved quickly on the mat, spinning the Fairview wrestler around to gain control. Bill's opponent slipped out from under him and threw Bill on the mat. They rolled several feet before Bill could regain his balance. Finally, Bill turned his man over and pinned

*Bill moved quickly on the mat, spinning
the Fairview wrestler around.*

him. He had won his first match!

Bill walked slowly to the bench.

"That's a workout," he said, taking a long, cool drink of water. He was through wrestling for the day. But there was still the rest of the team to cheer for.

Bill yelled for each of his teammates as the match worked its way up the weight divisions. In the final bout, Joe was pinned by his opponent, and Fairview won the match. But it had been a hard-earned victory for Fairview, and Coach Harding was pleased.

"That was a good first match," Coach Harding said in the locker room. "We did a few things well and a few things not so well. But we'll keep working at it, OK?"

"Yeah!" the squad shouted.

This really is a team, thought Bill. He

"That was a good first match,"
Coach Harding said.

changed clothes and was about to leave when Joe stopped him.

"You did well today," Joe said.

"I guess so," said Bill. "You did OK, too."

"But I lost," Joe said. "That guy really moved me around."

"Maybe you're just used to smaller guys," Bill said. "But you're strong. You'll do all right in this sport."

"Maybe," said Joe, with a trace of anger in his voice. "See you around."

"Yeah, see you."

Bill turned and watched Joe leave. The two boys were now teammates.

And teams are built on friendship, Bill thought, hopefully.

Lost and Found

A gentle breeze stirred the tall pines at the Mason Farm Golf Club. It was a Saturday afternoon in early June, a perfect day for golf.

John and Billy sat on the clubhouse steps, looking down the fairway at a foursome that had just teed off. One of the golfers hit a high iron shot that landed on the green. The next man hit his ball into the trees to the right of the green.

"Now, we're going to have to wait," John groaned.

"So what?" Billy said. "We get to sit a while longer, and I'd rather watch than carry."

"I'd rather play than watch," John said. But that was their problem — they didn't own their own clubs. The boys worked as caddies to earn enough money to buy golf clubs.

"Let's get going," Billy sighed as he saw the foursome move out of view. It was time to begin work. They each carried two bags to the first tee.

"Maybe by next June, we'll have some clubs," John said. After the golfers hit their drives, the boys followed slowly behind the group.

All of the golfers in the foursome were good, and that meant that Billy and John wouldn't have to spend all day looking for lost balls.

Pretty soon, the foursome came to the fifth hole. The fifth hole was a long par-five that had a hidden pond in the center of the fairway. From the tee, a golfer couldn't see the pond, but everybody at the Mason Farm Golf Club knew the water was there.

It was a hard shot to clear the pond, even for the best golfers at the club. "I hope they all make it," John whispered to Billy. Every Saturday, when they came to this hole, the boys spent a long time looking for lost balls. But once a ball was hit into the pond, it stayed there. The pond was deep, muddy, and bordered by tall reeds.

The golfers hit their tee shots

"This pond swallows golf balls."

straight down the fairway. Yet, when the group walked the course, there were only two golf balls on the fairway.

"We'd better start looking," Billy said. The caddies put down their bags and began circling the pond.

"See anything?" one of the golfers asked. Billy shook his head, but he kept on searching. After about five minutes, the golfers gave up and played provisional balls.

"It happens every time," one of the golfers said. "This pond swallows golf balls." He threw down a new ball and hit it towards the green.

"It was a brand-new ball," another golfer said to Billy. "I bet I lose two or three balls a month on this hole."

John looked at Billy with a wild gleam in his eyes. After the round was over, he grabbed Billy and took him to the caddy shack.

"We're going to have our clubs," John said.

"You're out of your mind. We didn't even get a tip today."

"That's because we're in the wrong business," said John. "We've been in the carrying business. But that's over. Now, we are in the lost-and-found business."

"What?"

"Today we carried the clubs of some of the best golfers we know, right?" John asked. "Right. And they lost two balls in the pond. Sometimes all four golfers can't find their tee shots. There must be hundreds of golf balls in that pond, and we're going to get them."

"I'm not going to jump into that pond," Billy said. "What about the mud, and what about snakes?"

"Did you ever *see* any snakes?" John asked.

"Everybody says there are snakes," said Billy.

"That's a chance we'll have to take."

A heavy rain closed the Mason Farm Golf Club the following day, but John asked Billy to meet him at the course anyway.

John had brought bathing suits, ball retrievers, a rake, and two large sacks to put the balls in. They stood at the edge of the pond and watched the rain make ripples on the surface.

"I don't think I can go in," Billy said, his lips quivering.

John grabbed the rake and walked to the edge of the water. He reached out as far as he could with the rake, then pulled. Five or six shiny golf balls rolled towards him.

67

"It's a gold mine!" John shouted. He pulled the rake in again, and five more balls floated into view.

"I'm still scared," Billy said. "But I'm not *that* scared."

John and Billy circled the lake, pulling in balls with the rake and placing them in their sacks.

"We've got to go farther in," John said.

The muddy bottom felt just as disgusting as they expected. John and Billy trembled at first, but went deeper into the lake. They used their toes, the rake, and the ball retrievers to scoop balls off the bottom of the pond. Soon both sacks were full.

"We've got over two hundred golf balls," John said. "New clubs, here we come!"

Then, through the rain, the boys saw

*John circled the lake, pulling in balls
with the rake.*

the manager of the golf course. He was driving his jeep towards them. He drove to the edge of the pond and got out.

"You kids know you're not allowed on the course if it's closed," he said, looking very angry. "You're trespassing." Then he saw the two sacks of balls.

"Cleaning out the pond, huh? Well, you'd better come to my office tomorrow." And with that, he picked up both sacks, tossed them into the jeep, and drove away. The boys stood in the heavy rain and looked at each other.

"Do you think we'll still be able to caddy?" asked Billy.

John looked at him and shook his head. "We'll have to wait and see."

The next morning, John and Billy walked slowly into the manager's office.

"I've been thinking it over," the manager said. "It's true, you shouldn't have been on the course yesterday, but you did do me a favor. Usually, I pay people to clean out the pond."

The manager walked behind his desk, picking up two sets of golf clubs that were in pretty good shape.

"How about an even trade?" the manager said.

"The golf balls for the clubs?" asked John.

"That's right."

"You've got a deal!" both boys shouted.

"One more thing," the manager said. "You won't be fooling around in the pond again, will you?"

"No, sir."

"Good. Now, why don't you go try out your new clubs? The course is practically

71

John hit his tee shot towards the fairway.

empty today."

A few minutes later, John and Billy were on the first tee. They played the first four holes quickly. Then, they came to the fifth hole.

"Well, here goes," John said, hitting his tee shot towards the fairway. It looked like a pretty good shot. Billy's tee shot also looked like it would make the fairway. But when the boys walked down the fairway, their balls were missing.

The hidden pond had struck again.

Showboat

I have to admit that Bob Owens is a great basketball player. He drives and shoots better than anybody on the team, and when the game is close, Bob likes to have the ball.

But that's our problem—he doesn't like to share the ball.

Well, Jack Brown, our center, called a team meeting today for everyone except Bob.

"I don't want Bob there," Jack had said. "The meeting is about him."

At first, the meeting was very quiet. We didn't know what to say about Bob, and we all felt funny about having a secret meeting. It just didn't seem like something a team should do.

"We've got to do something about Showboat," Jack finally said. We called Bob "Showboat" because he liked to show off and be the star.

"What can we do?" I asked. I don't get to play very much, but I could tell pretty easily that Bob was a ball-hog.

"Showboat doesn't pass to us," Jack said. "Coach Ronson tells him to pass, but he never does. He just shoots."

"But he hits his shots," said Hermy,

"Showboat doesn't pass to us, he just shoots."

our guard. "Without Bob, we wouldn't be too tough."

Jack threw a towel at the locker.

"That's just the point. If Bob played *with* us, we could be a great basketball team."

Everybody realized that Jack was probably right. If we *all* played together, no one could touch us.

"What if we just don't give him the ball for a while?" Jack suggested. And that's what we did.

The next night, the Cougars came to our gym, bringing all their fans. The place was packed to the top of the bleachers, because everyone knows that when the Cougars play the Raiders, sparks fly.

Jack reminded everybody about our plan, and right away, we put it to work. Jeremy brought the ball up court, using a slow dribble to study the Cougar defense. Bob broke free on the baseline, but Jeremy slipped a bounce pass in the middle to Jack instead. Jack spun to his right and flipped the ball to Craig, who took a jump shot. *Swish*!

Things fell apart after that, though. Everybody tried so hard *not* to pass the ball to Bob that we had more turnovers than shots. At the end of the first quarter, we trailed the Cougars 17–5.

"What's the matter with you guys?" Bob said on the bench. "I've been open the whole time."

"We didn't see you," Jack mumbled.

Coach Ronson knew what was going on, and at halftime, he told us how he felt.

"You guys are awful. You work out problems in practice, not in ball games." He went into his office, slamming the door.

"I want to know what's going on," Bob said.

"All right," said Jack. "You're a ball-hog, Showboat, and we don't like it."

"Is that what you think? I just want to win."

"But you play by yourself," said Jack.

"No I don't!" Bob said. He looked around angrily at the rest of us. Then he stood up. "You guys can play without me. I quit."

When Coach Ronson came out of his office, Jack told him what happened.

"Do the best you can," Coach Ronson said.

But I knew the Cougars were going to have the time of their lives. And sure enough, they destroyed us that night.

It was a glum practice the next after-noon. Not only had the Cougars run us

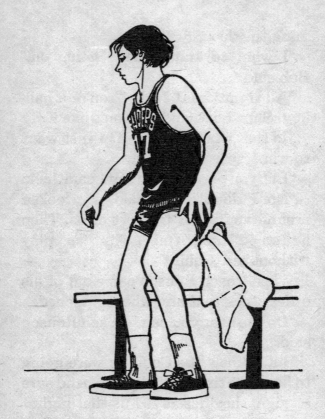

"You guys can play without me. I quit."

out of our own gym, but our little plan had also cost us our best player. Now, we had a weak team without a consistent scorer. I hoped Bob would come back, but I knew it was best not to say anything.

We lost our next three games, and, although I got to play more, losing is never much fun. During one game, I saw Bob in the stands. I could tell he was going crazy not playing.

A couple of days later, he came to practice, looking very tired.

"I've been doing a lot of thinking," he said. "Coach Ronson said I should talk to you."

"So talk," Jack said sharply.

"I love basketball," Bob began. "I get so wrapped up in it that I don't know anybody else is alive."

He paused, looking at his sneakers.

"I guess that's been obvious. I can't stand losing, but I really can't stand not playing and watching us lose. I can change the way I play. All I need is a chance."

It was Jack's move. If he said OK, Bob would be back on the team.

"I want to be a winner," Jack said. "We've got a few games left...let's take them all."

"You mean it?" Bob asked.

"But as a team," Jack said.

At practice that day, Bob was everywhere. He hustled on defense and passed the ball to everybody. Gradually, we adjusted to the change in Bob's game. For the first time, we were playing like a team.

The next week, we had another game against the Cougars. Bob had something to say before the game.

*He hustled on defense and passed the ball
to everybody.*

"I used to think I was the Showboat.
Let's show the Cougars that when this
team works together, we're all Show-
boats!"

The Cougars, I am proud to say,
never knew what hit them.

Born to Run

Fred Murdock searched in his coat pockets, his pants, and his shirt.

"Where's my lunch money?" he yelled. Finally, inside his notebook, he found a five-dollar bill. Clutching his money, Fred waddled towards his favorite part of the school, the lunch room.

He was very hungry, but this wasn't exactly a news item at Cary High School. It was well known that Fred Murdock loved to eat. Huffing and puffing, he ran to the cafeteria as fast as he could. This wasn't too fast because Fred was very, very heavy. In fact, Fred was fat.

Panting, Fred stood in line, eyeing the menu.

"Two lunches," he said, hoping that it would be enough. Today, they offered turkey with dressing, mashed potatoes, green beans, salad, rolls, peach cobbler, and milk.

The cashier didn't show any surprise at Fred's order. He always ate two lunches. Sometimes he ate three.

"Sit over here," Steve called. Steve was fond of watching Fred pack it away. "Just two lunches today, Fred?"

Fred always ate two lunches.

he asked.

"Yeah," Fred said, forking a lump of mashed potatoes. "I had a good breakfast."

After eating his lunches, Fred usually went to the playground to watch softball. He liked sports and had tried to play them, but he had always been too slow. So he gave up trying to play and just watched.

Fred also liked to watch girls, but he was too shy to ask anyone out.

One day at lunch, Fred noticed something strange. Alice Johnson, one of the heavier girls at Cary High School, began jogging around the playing field. Alice looked sharp in a new running outfit, running shoes, and a towel around her neck.

"She's trying to kill herself," Fred said. "She's almost as heavy as I am."

Alice ran very slowly around the field four times. Then she walked around twice more. When she finished, Fred walked over to her.

"What's going on?" Fred asked.

"What do you mean?" said Alice.

"Why are you jogging?"

"Jogging makes me feel good," she said. "It's helping me drop a few pounds, too."

"Lose weight?" Fred wondered. "Why do you want to do that?"

"You ought to know, Fred. Who wants to go out with a blob?"

After school, Fred thought about Alice. Her words rang in his ears. *Who wants to go out with a blob?*

Fred watched Alice every day. He noticed that she ran longer distances, at a faster pace. He also noticed how pretty Alice really was.

Alice ran very slowly around the field.

"How much weight have you lost?" Fred asked a couple of weeks later.

"Almost twenty pounds. I've got a long way to go, but I'm getting there."

"I'll say," Fred said.

Alice laughed as she wiped her forehead with her towel.

"Have you ever thought about jogging, Fred?"

"Yeah," Fred said. "I've thought about it. In fact, you've inspired me to start a program today."

"Really?" asked Alice. "How many lunches did you have today?"

"Two."

"You call that sensible eating, Fred?"

"No, but it was all I could afford."

Alice didn't laugh at Fred's attempt at humor.

"This is a joke that's on you," she said, grabbing her things to leave.

Fred raced after her.

"Alice, there's a dance this weekend. Would you like to go with me?"

"I already have a date, but thanks anyway, Fred."

Fred sat down on a bench, feeling stunned and very much alone. He walked home slowly.

The next day, he walked into the lunch room, carrying a small travel bag.

"I would like one apple and one banana," Fred told the cashier.

The cashier nearly choked. "Are you all right, Fred?"

"Never better."

The lunch room grew very still. What was going on? Fred Murdock did not buy lunch. Later, the students at Cary High School had another surprise. They saw Fred, in a pair of faded

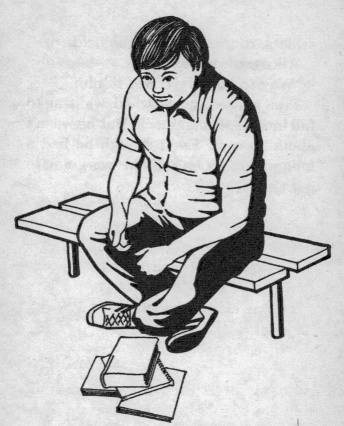

*Fred sat down on a bench, feeling
very much alone.*

sweats, running around the field.

Alice cruised past Fred.

"Way to go!" she called to him.

Fred panted and coughed, wanting to fall into a soft hammock. But he wasn't about to quit. Even though he had a long way to go, he knew he was going to get there.